Cut to Size

Sally Cattell

Cover Design by Luke Buxton | www.lukebuxton.com

I dedicate this book to all who believe in
secret communication between trees.

Prologue

An Encounter. A cry for help.

I have had enough. My head aches with all those domineering and grasping hands. My foot sends shooting pains each time I am forced to connect with the ground. I confess this room is magnificent of which I share an insignificant part. Elaborate furnishings and decor, which only make me feel depressed, a shadow of my former glory.

'Michael, Michael,' I murmur. 'Can you hear me? All I can hear is His Lordship snoring.'

Of course I hear you, I am always here when you call.

'I can't go on anymore. I am so tired.'

Yours has been a long journey, because you are special. Tell me how you feel.

'I don't know really. Shall I tell you about today or when I first wound up here.'

Today might be helpful. Take your time.

'Oak has called on you for thousands of years – especially when he's needed to understand more. I still don't get it that you will talk with me now and no one can see or hear us doing so. It makes me sad remembering what I used to be – attached to magnificent Oak.'

The Angel didn't speak and I was aware of the silence all around, no hint of traffic which was something I suppose. I began to feel a comforting tingle which had nothing to do with the warmth of the room. Angel touched my head. It was like a release from all my sadness; rather like the feeling that swept through us on that momentous day, high up on a hill, thousands of years ago.

'The morning was misty to start with and then the sun came out. I enjoyed our early morning walk in Green Park, seeing nephews, some as tall as I was many years ago. In fact when His Honour sat down and me with him, I could see right opposite to one who connected with me. A breeze ruffled his glory as it used to do for Oak. His Honour made a harrumph sound looking at his watch, which meant we had to leave. It was as though he would have preferred to stay. Quite unexpectedly I was lifted up and felt the touch of creation, and its myriad of textures, reminding me of what it used to feel like, the joy of being alive. His Honour murmured, 'beautiful, beautiful', at least that's what I thought he said. I so wanted to stay awhile but that was not to be. Not in his schedule anyway. We returned to his apartment and the breakfast room where I was deposited next to a highly polished affair, subtlety joined in strips hardly noticeable to the human eye. I was leaning against a distant cousin or so I believed. Above, on this cousin's surface, there was a weird smell of burnt fish wafting my way which His Honour was imbibing, and following this a strong smell of grass which I couldn't identify.

'After this he took me into the library (I know that is what it is called because he mentions the word many times to visitors). The shelves, although related to me, somehow were quiet and although this was a room I loved I felt them looking down on me, a mere strip not worth bothering about. His Honour collected some papers and a diary, and we went into the main hall.

'There he summoned his chauffeur driven car. He sat in the back seat and placed me into a clip near the back armrest, upright, where I could see through the window; buildings, bridges, taxis, two story busses, other vehicles, and all manner of people before our journey ended at the House of Parliament steps. The journey all too short because I liked the smell of leather and the deep purr the engine made. Then I was whisked away up some steps and into a raised seating area with His Honour's palm clamped around my head; aware of angry voices giving me a headache. It was horrible. It grew worse as he banged me up and down on the floor. Then people on either side of the seating began shouting. Suddenly I was marched out and around which made me dizzy. What did that mean? Michael?'

It sounds, being the Houses of Parliament, that there was a vote and I know, in this case, it resulted in a vote of no confidence in the Prime Minister. She had to resign. I imagine everyone present was airing their views.

'The noise was shattering and everyone was shouting.'

You prefer the quiet?

'Peace is more like it .The day deteriorated from then on. I feel more at home in the park watching my magnificent cousins swaying in the breeze. They are almost as important as I used to be.'

Why do you want to be important?

'I don't know. I can't forget how wonderful it made me feel being part of the largest, most beautiful tree on the hillside. Now look at me. I feel so ashamed.'

This will be your final chance to understand your role in the world. Is there anything else you want to say?

'It's a question. What does Brexit mean?'

He that goeth forth weeping bearing the seed for sowing,
Shall come home with shouts of joy, bringing his sheaves with him.
Psalm 126:6

Chapter 1

My life began in the dark but I remember one day seeing a spot of light. I knew then that I was important. And as I grew I looked around. It was a sight to see. There on the hillside were other species doing the same, growing towards the light. I felt strong nevertheless and realised why I felt strong. Important if you like. I was different. Others jockeyed for space but I commanded respect, my position on the hillside was way more significant. The higher I grew the more those around struck me as expendable.

How wrong was I.

It seemed I lived a charmed life, nothing got in my way. From dawn to dusk, rain, sun or high wind my frame was magnificent. In fact I relished my superiority. Some days I could see for miles, on others mist clouded my vista. Those of my ilk have covered the earth from time immemorial, whilst I embrace all below me.

To my left there are some saplings struggling whereas I have many fruits. My canopy spreads gently housing all who alight, their feathery wings hidden among abundant foliage. Those creatures who inhabit my hillside within and below know their place. I see the babbling stream with its rocks and weeds surrounded by yellow and blue flowers lifting their hues when the sun comes up, all very pleasing to the eye, where youngsters paddle and pick the wild flowers. This is my home and land where I thrive in all weathers, especially the crisp air – I breathe that in with relish.

The sunshine can burn and dry out the soil but my reservoirs beneath the earth are sufficient. Nothing harms me now that I am fully grown.

As the mist lifts I make out the city glistening in the crisp air and feel the small rodents burrowing at my feet. Over to my right, lower down, the refugee family has been decimated and rightly so, they were of inferior lineage. There are men and carts coming in my direction probably to gather my fruits, certainly nothing to be alarmed about. 'Stay, stay,' I whisper to each limb. All is as it should be. Someone is rustling my lower branches – I can feel his cheeky touch but cannot see him clearly. Swaying you around. 'Don't worry you will not snap I promise you.' The morning haze is lifting and I begin to feel concern. I beseech the heavens to intervene, but there is no answer. I can feel a rope around me, feet climbing my outer shield and a hook. A terrible noise attacking my branches and looking down I feel something leaning, propped up half way around my trunk. A person clambering up to my head. I can't make out what he is calling to the others on the ground, but a rope is tied around and thrown down, and another one in the opposite direction. Surely my majesty will deter any more insults. Can't they see how beautiful I am. My feathery friends fly away as I am stripped bare, my beautiful limbs gone. Then the pain as my body receives forceful blows and I fall down losing consciousness. Am I going to die? I dreamed about the time crowds of people came to hear a man speak. He sat under my branches whilst the crowd sat further down the hillside. I listened to what he said. It appeared to be strange as after he left the crowd stayed discussing what they heard. Eventually they all left too. Something he said was rather odd.... that the meek would inherit the earth. I could see him now and hear some of his words wafting around in my thoughts. Blessed; yes that was the word he kept using. There are arms and hands surrounding me, pulling, sliding, and tipping me, Ooh help! Waking up, I am being slotted into a cart with my canopy in disarray. The cart is bumping along until we reach a smooth road. I am being taken away from my home, my beautiful hillside. The sun goes down and still the journey continues where all I can see is the sky and the first stars peeping out. This is the worst day of my life. The ground is changing now, more uneven than earlier. I see walls to the right and left, giving me a horrible feeling of being closed in. I try not to panic, keeping my eyes on the sky until that too is gone and then we stop.

The cart stayed there for two whole days and then the pulling and sliding began all over again. I cried out but no one came to my aid. So, this is what it is to die...I am all alone. Daylight floods around, now that those on top of me have been hauled away. I can breathe again. Arms hoist me up and I can see many different logs piled every which way, their colours unfamiliar. Hoisted higher the sounds are far from friendly. Harsh commands come from men dressed in brightly coloured clothes with weapons by their sides. Rich looking footwear strapped to their legs and bright shiny head gear covering their ears; barking orders to those of lesser importance. There is a smell of dust, oil and I know not what, as all around my being a tool is rubbing away my distinctive outer glory. Surely there has been a mistake. I am better than all the others in here. Some lying down and some leaning up against each other; measured into long and short pieces. Suddenly my lower half is sawn off. Oh the pain. How degrading.

All I hear is cursing, no feathery friends anywhere only distant cousins looking frightened but like me unable to be heard. I notice we are shunted to different areas according to our size, then loaded back on a cart to who knows where? I see many smaller cut offs being nailed cross wise to their uprights. How awful! I see the hammers and see the shudders. Dreading what was apparently going to happen to me. I blocked out the sounds and images, my tears reflecting back on the hillside where I grew; trying to hold onto my freedom that once was my world. Wild flowers lifting their heads to the rain and sunshine; my feathery friends and all that sheltered within my limbs. Would I ever see such beauty again? Would I ever wake up from this nightmare?

My distinct strong covering is being stripped and falling, falling onto the ground. I am left naked breathing in bitter tannins that have served me well; no nasty predators ever broke through my protection. The pain slowly travels throughout my body. In all these years no fungi ever invaded me – they knew their place, feeding my roots. Now what is happening? I can't bear any more pain. It's as though I have been singled out for such violent treatment and still I live! Stripped from all my glory for what end? Between my slashed and splintered body smothered with vile smelling oil; I cry out as I am finally split in two. My lower half has had the same treatment. We are together loaded onto a cart with ropes and iron spikes. Transported into a building not far away with others. Then tipped out onto a yard bruised and desperate. I hear voices giving commands. Smell food cooking and try to make sense of it all; in spite of the humiliation and pain. The men with tools seemed to be in charge. Slaves were ordered to sort the pile of logs of which I was one into sizes. There was a lot of activity and sawdust everywhere. I could hear shouting coming from a building nearby. Leading off from this yard there were numerous stalls in which horses were tethered. Two men with helmets, capes and swords appeared leading a horse each, fitting purple capes across the horses' backs. Hands checked harnesses as an order was given to mount, the soldiers' helmets glistening as the riders edged their way outside. I now realised, these were Roman soldiers. They were the law.

By now I was lifted up and I could see young boys peering through one of the iron latticed walls. They were shooed away. Slaves carried me and my cross beam out of the yard. They were told to wait. I didn't deserve this treatment. Wasn't it clear who I was and where I grew up? My magnificent branches, my sturdy trunk, my delicious fruits. I was the greatest tree on the hillside far away in Galilee. The noise coming from the street was deafening. Then I saw the back of the prisoner above us.

Steps led to a gold coloured chair where a man in rich clothes sat talking to a prisoner who stood silently and never said a word. It was hard to hear above the yelling crowd but eventually the prisoner was led away. Maybe it was the way he stood or his simple robe but I had that strange feeling he was familiar. It seemed a long time before anything else happened and I was beginning to feel dizzy what with the heat and the slaves fidgeting as they held me upright. I heard carts rumbling past. Children's voices playing and the oddest sound, like bleating, as the yelling quietened down. People from far away were arriving for what I couldn't imagine. I glimpsed two men in the crowd wearing costly robes stirring up the people. They seemed very important as their head dresses and robes were a brilliant blue and sparkling with precious stones.

I couldn't understand any of it and what was more – why was all this happening to me and the silent prisoner.

...do not boast over your branches. If you do boast, remember it is not you that supports the root, but the root that supports you.
Romans 11:18

Chapter 2

The man stood in the courtyard overlooking crowds of angry people. His hands tied behind his back, bruises and dirt streaking his face; a circlet of myrtle pressed onto his head from which thorns tore at his flesh creating rivulets of blood. He was being accused of something by those dressed in long robes of finery. Another man of fine purple robes as those of a king, ordered a bowl of water where he washed his hands. Why? I had no idea. Looking down at the bottom of the steps the crowd were yelling and punching the air with their fists, 'Blasphemy, blasphemy'. This disturbed everyone there, not least the many more guards who appeared whilst he dried his hands on a white cloth, turning away from the crowd.

In spite of my humiliation it felt nothing compared to the man with the bruised face. He was bustled over to where I was watching from saying very little. All of a sudden I remembered his voice from a time past when he stood under my wonderful canopy speaking to the crowd with gentle authority. They had gathered lower down the hillside, hushed to hear his every word. For a moment I forgot my pain as he looked right through me and then looked up above the roof to the hillside beyond. A blue mantle was thrown across his shoulders and he was pushed back to the centre of the courtyard.

There appeared to be a choice given to the crowd as to which of two men they wanted released. I was astonished as the crowd seemed to want someone else. What with the yelling, the heat and the strange smells all around I hardly had time to ponder before my cut off base was split again, smoothed roughly and balanced across my being higher up. A spike was driven through it to me and I felt the inadequate resin pouring from me; attempting to heal. My separate parts calmed each other, welcoming our join although clumsy in its outrage. Soothed by the resin's aroma I wondered what else I would have to endure. Similar actions were taking place all around. 'Bang, Bang' the spikes went in to others. However, being smaller in stature they were being bundled carefully with ropes and carried away by men in shiny helmets.

I was dragged out of the yard and down amongst the shouting people. The crowd parted as the bruised and bleeding man was roughly shoved back against me. His arms lifted around my cross beam, his hands clenching either side. Two riders on horseback jostled the crowd away, their helmets glistening in the sun, their short cloaks fluttering, their golden sandals urging their mounts to keep walking. Every so often people who came too close were threatened by swords. As we progressed along, the jarring of my base on the rough ground sent pain throughout my being. He tried to carry me but only collapsed onto his knees. I was too heavy for him. He raised himself up and kept going as best he could but the jarring was so painful on that dreadful walk. Some areas were very narrow so that the crowd were pushed against market carts. The riders taking it in turn to lead and follow behind. I felt his hands shift closer to his head trying to lift me so I didn't bump and jar his back but he couldn't hold me there and fell to his knees again. The riders looked at a loss as what to do. At this point a woman pushed forward, kneeling down beside him. She had a cloth that had a refreshing aroma as she wiped his bruised face crying, 'Yesu, Yesu,' before she was hustled away. It was obvious Yesu could not get up and carry me. The guard on horseback shouted something towards the crowd and a dark skinned man from another country, at least I guessed that he was because I had never seen someone of his colour; came forward and picked up my lower end, lifting me up to waist height with no trouble at all; he was very tall and strong and began singing a sad song in a language I had never heard before. The jeering stopped as the crowd fell back. We moved along cobbled stones, the stranger's voice low and rich between sobs.

I could feel Yesu determined to carry on in spite of being at the end of his endurance. And me? I was relieved of bruising and pain rising up and down my body. We continued along the cobbles in this fashion until we came to a gate – here the crowd thinned out and sounded far more subdued. Ahead was a midden from which unpleasant smells emanated, surrounding us. I tried thinking of the pleasant air on the hillside where I grew up. How I loved the tiny creatures climbing up my tough casing then chasing each other along my canopy. I remembered sometimes it swayed in the breeze bringing much chattering. A hop skip and a jump nibbling my fruits. How I loved sheltering these little ones keeping them from harm.

All gone now. At those times I felt such happiness pouring out to all those who flew among my swaying arms whilst those who sheltered below would need no reminding how I cared for each one. What a strange thought to be having as we struggled across the rubbish to the allotted area. At last we came to a halt. I was lifted off Yesu and laid down on the ground. Yesu watched as ropes were attached to me and tethered to spikes. The dark man stumbled back the way we came; roughly ordered to leave us. Everyone was shunted down to the bottom of the midden. We were alone apart from those in charge clearing away rubbish. I could see the sky and wondered what would happen next. A small ledge was hammered into my body. Later, I realised it was placed so that Yesu was forced to bend his knees, and so they could nail his feet to it. As I watched, Yesu's mantle was whisked away. He was pushed down to lie on top of me his arms stretched out and a nail hammered into his wrists. His hands alongside my cross beam the reverse of before. Then the ropes were grasped as I was positioned into a hole in the ground firmly with a thump. Between bouts of pain and sadness I was amazed how strong I could be. As I looked around Yesu was silent. Two other men were also strung up similar to Yesu but their arms were tied to the cross beam and their feet left to hang. I saw women stricken with grief and watched the sky as it darkened. Those in charge lit a fire and passed Yesu's robe amongst themselves.

As daylight faded, I heard a rumble as though a storm was about to descend on us. It was then I had the most peaceful feeling flowing through my body as blood dripped downwards. It seems to be passing from Yesus' wonderful hands. His blood healing my shattered self. How can this be? He is suffering but I do not anymore. The storm arrived suddenly and there was an eerie glow all around. Two women were weeping as they held each other. Is one Yesu's mother? Yesu calls out to the man standing next to them. Time seems to stand still as the flames of the fire flicker this and that way, the rubbish is blowing all around us and it is then I hear Yesu call out in such despair. Not long after he cried, 'It is finished'. Lightening filled the sky. Yesu's breathing fades as he moved his head against me and then he was still. 'Oh my what now?' I make out several figures in the darkness coming towards us carrying wooden steps which are leant against me. Those in charge have gone to seek shelter taking Yesu's cloak with them. The darkness is very strange. The flames of the fire have died down and the wind has become even angrier. I feel the nails being pulled out very slowly from Yesu's hands; the points being bent back to their original shape. His body is released, wrapped and hurried away. I am alone in my shock as I hear words passed from figure to figure. 'Hurry Passover must be done before.' Eventually they too left the midden. I am superfluous.

No you're not.

'Who's there? I cannot see you.'

True, but I'm here to help. I am the Angel, Michael.

'How can you help me? Look how low I've fallen! No one cares or wants me.'

On the contrary you will be much in demand for centuries to come.

'How can you know that? My life is over.'

You were especially chosen by God.

'To do what? Dragged along the city streets, and ending up here on this midden with a man nailed to me – I feel so ashamed.'

Not just any man. He didn't do anything wrong. He was God's son.

'What's that to do with me?' There seemed to be a long silence before the spirit spoke again.

With his hands he made you from the beginning of the universe. Didn't you feel your pain going when his blood washed over you? You and your species will do remarkable things 'till the end of time.

I was quiet for a long time trying to understand what the spirit told me. Dawn was breaking up the shadows. 'Are you still here?'

Yes.

'But I don't want to do remarkable things as you call it. I want to be beautiful as before.' Another long silence stretched out before the spirit spoke again.

You will be beautiful again in a different way. Your body has been touched by the most precious hands on earth and when you understand that you are a child of the living spirit – you will no longer hear the voice of the world. Reject the deceiver and you will attain the 'Clarity of Truth'. I must leave you now but whenever you call - I'll be there. You will not die providing you listen to the spirit within you.

'I will live?' He didn't answer. I felt a soft breeze wafting over me and a sense of calm. Two days and two nights I was left there without Yesu, hearing the groans of the men either side of me. They are taking much longer to die. The storm passes and the hot wind returns, blowing rubbish every which way. Am I being left here to rot? I am so confused but not in pain anymore. I just feel awkward.

As another day dawns I see streams of people carrying their possessions, herding sheep, and goats alongside carts loaded up with family members. All jostling one another vying for position through the gate. Children play games between the carts, annoying worried parents admonishing them to stay close or they may get lost. I presumed all these people came up from the countryside to join in with the 'Passover' feast. I had heard this earlier from pilgrims calling to each other on arrival. Now they were returning to their villages, farms, and work places many days away.

Where was Yesu? Who had taken him away? And why did he have to die? And more to the point, why was I chosen for this to happen to? I no longer felt afraid and pondered on what the angel told me. And I remember thinking what will be will be, but wished I had some idea as to what would happen next. I know I didn't feel grand anymore but in a strange way I understood something way above my imaginings had taken place. Here I stood above the city as a symbol for all to see.

At last an ox and cart were coming towards me with men who released me from the ground, took away the ropes and slid me onto the cart. We trundled away from the hill, past many buildings, along cobbled streets and crowds of people, none of which took any notice. As we approached a shed a man came out to greet the cart. He was dressed very differently to those I had previously seen. He wore a large brown apron over a loose sleeved shirt, his sleeves rolled up and in his hand he carried some food which he held out to the oxen. I guessed his apron was made of tanned leather from one of my close relatives and that he was in charge of a carpenters shop nearby. This was to be my home for some time. Most of what happened here is a blur but I do remember being treated with respect. Perhaps even love.

...Have you not known?...the Lord is the everlasting God the Creator of The ends of the earth...He gives power to the faint and to him who has no might He increases strength.
Isaiah 40:28-29

Chapter 3

I remember being separated from my cross beam and was astonished watching that part of me being whittled into small objects, each smoothed into a shine. I was so immersed in what was happening that all thoughts of misery took a backward step. Instead I found it amazing that part of me should be moulded into small replicas of the shape I had become. Some had delicate chains attached to them and placed into small boxes. I realised much later the significance of these objects as I saw them everywhere, not only made from me but all sorts of materials; some man made, some dug out of the ground, but none from my ancestry.

As for myself, I was planed down, measured, polished and sent across the sea, many seas as it turned out. And for centuries I was left in peace within large buildings where music soared above the people below. It was uplifting listening to all sorts of instruments especially as time moved along. Enormous pipes were installed where a person sat in front of this massive instrument using their feet as well as their hands. Pushing knobs, buttons, stops and keys, creating music which soared in majesty around the building. I had never heard such a sound as the notes which echoed around the dome just above me. Time rolled by. Many centuries I think and I became used to being just a beam. Many times I called on my Angel Michael for help and each time he talked to me I gradually thought less about the past and my glory. I somehow grew less afraid for my future. I lost interest in dominating all around me. My pride had taken a tumble and in its place I was less obsessed with myself, humbled if you like. I think my fears became less as I thought about the healing I received out of the tremendous pain at that crucifixion (as Michael called it), all those years ago. My angel seemed to be in touch with Yesu although I never saw Him again. I wondered if this was to be my ending; but according to Michael it was not. This place, this cathedral, was a mere resting spot before what was to come.

But I am getting ahead of myself. There is so much to tell of awful behaviours, as to how lives changed, wars raged, customs differed and yet the aims were the same, control and power; far removed from the teachings of Yesu when He spoke to the crowds beneath my branches. It seems nothing changes from what happened in Jerusalem all those years ago. These are my impressions.

Clothes down the centuries altered. Language too, most I had little idea about except as I watched the ritual repeated (I now know) it was called chanting by those wearing cloaks of black, sometimes with hoods covering their heads. It was uplifting, the music swelling through these vast buildings and peaceful until one day everything changed. A knight on horseback rode up the centre aisle wearing a rich cloak studded with precious stones and fur. Hanging by his side was a sword encrusted with what looked like blood. On that particular day everything altered. Where once there was order now it was chaos. Where I had witnessed the rich and powerful, even Kings and Queens in attendance, now no one like that came to the cathedral. They were replaced with the poor, the homeless, the sick, and those souls who no one cared about; all of these rushed into the cathedral for sanctuary. There was absolute panic at the sound of steel crashing, screams and oaths. I saw people stripped and dragged before the alter, cut down, their heads speared by pikes. I could smell burning and found myself dislodged from on high, left lying on the ground. Everything happened so fast there was confusion as smoke was billowing around and still the clatter of steel, horses' hooves and general mayhem surrounded where I lay. This is where I finish up! Desperately I called on my Angel. 'What is to become of me?' But there was silence.

The night came early because it was winter and so it wasn't until the next day that I saw what had become of the cathedral. It was very cold and I watched the most beautiful sight of fluffy white sparkling drops falling from the sky. Where it lay was like a blanket covering the ravages of the cathedral as if it had never been. Myself included. At last Micheal came.

You called, Oak.

'So this is what I have become. Battered and bruised lying in this white blanket. No use to anyone; Just left here to rot!'

The beautiful flakes you see are soft and quiet. It is called snow. Nothing to be alarmed about. And you are wrong Oak. You have far to travel yet before your final destination.

'Don't try to soft soap me. Over the years I have seen many things, heard many languages, learnt various words but I have never been in a fire and almost destroyed. The smell is still around and it is very cold lying here. The only good thing is the quiet. I am a broken and bruised lump. How can I do anything worthwhile now? My cross beam was cut up to make goblets, bowls and small crosses. I saw it all. Since then I have noticed crosses of all sizes, some made of gold and of silver and some of other metals. Knights in armour wore them stitched into their robes; bright red. They were very large. Even flags were fluttering with the symbol. None realised that I was used by Yesu so long ago. So what does it mean?'

Because of Yesu and His teaching a religion has spread far and wide, a spiritual awakening if you like. The cross being the symbol of knights, Kings, and ordinary people. It will reach down in time where people will be known as Christians. The knight you saw in the knave was a woman.

'Are you sure?'

Yes. If you had looked carefully she was quite small and very young. She led an army because of her visions. Soldiers believed what she said. And she gave her life - because of the voices she heard believing they were from God. No one could persuade her otherwise. They burnt her at the stake, calling her a heretic because she was female and not important; just a simple peasant girl who ignored all the protocols regarding her sex. She is now in her saviour's arms for all eternity.

It took me some time to digest this information, before I blurted out, 'Wasn't she frightened?'

Of course she was but the message she carried was more important to her than her life. Oh Oak think back to Yesu's crucifixion. Yesu didn't die — He lives on through the centuries. He gave His life so all who believe in him should have everlasting life if they carry His words in their hearts. She is one among many who will lose their lives in Yesu's service throughout time.

'What makes people fight all the time? I've seen people have their heads cut off! Not to mention violence of all kinds, all in the name of this religion.'

I lay there for a while feeling the soft flakes wafting around me unable to grasp my situation. Thinking back to the time Yesu stood underneath my canopy preaching to the people, the warmth in the air; how remote it all was from me now lying on the ground battered and bruised once again. I supposed people broke Yesu's rules?

No, that is not Yesu's message. There are no rules.

'How did you know what I was thinking?'

I am a spirit. I know what you think. That is my sole vocation to hear you call and to know your thoughts. I am your personal guardian.

'So if there are no rules how do the people know what is right or wrong?'

There is just one emotion for all to remember and that is to love each other whoever you meet. The other point is not to judge others but to forgive. The measure you give will be the measure you will receive. Maybe not right now but at a later time.

'This is all a bit above me as I lie on the ground cold and wet.'

Think back to when Yesu was nailed to you. How did you feel?

'To begin with I was in pain and terrified but as time wore on I felt a great healing peace. My pain no longer occupied my thoughts instead I thought about Yesu and that he didn't deserve to die.'

So hold onto that peace. He has important things for you to do.

'How can that be? I am lying on the ground covered in snowflakes so that if a person was to walk my way I'd be hidden and no doubt they'd trip over me?'

Rest awhile and you will see.

And having said that he left. It was very cold and I began to panic. No matter what Angel said it was like lying in a tomb. The day wore on and the darkness fell and I tried to think about the earlier times when nothing impeded my happiness; when I stood tall, strong and beautiful. I thought of sunshine past, wild flowers, birds and little animals; of Yesu talking to the crowds who came to listen at His feet. Was I the product of His design? Did those hands fling the stars into the heavens? I can see Him now striding towards me, looking up to my top most branches and standing right in front of me before he turned to address the crowds. Am I to understand that those healing hands created all that man could see? Did He have a plan for me? I pondered on this thought for a while in my semi-delirium.

The night wore on and at last, as dawn broke, I could hear voices and the clattering sound of tools cracking the ice around. The snow had become frozen solid, and as the dawn spread, the sky cleared allowing me to see the heavens once again with some stars still shimmering. In the distance I heard chanting which held my attention. Lots of voices as if they were walking towards me and the devastated cathedral. That night is etched into my memory. What with Angel and all he said, the breath of horses coming in puffs, the carts, the weak sun melting the ice, the slosh of cart wheels and the feeling of damp going right through me. Within a short while men were retrieving objects; some charred, some burnt beyond recognition, and some covered in ash. I was lifted up and saw an enormous gold cross being wrapped in cloth and carried away; myself being lowered into a cart with other beams and assorted artefacts, also a lectern scarred and the intricate surrounding of a pulpit and a much charred door with its iron handle. I felt motion, and heard the clatter of hooves, voices and cries and eventually I was housed in a large shed where I saw wood shavings. I wondered what would happen and how long I would be here. Where was my next destination? And will Angel continue to come if I call?

I had been so long in the cathedral and had learnt many words because of the repetition of those chants and because of the glorious music which soared to the ceiling as many people sang. I learnt later that whatever the language some words were similar and often meant the same things. The unfamiliar words were so often sung in my new home that I could grasp some understanding. Although growing in knowledge and language none to my mind helped my situation. I suppose some would envy me as I travelled the world and crossed seas but I couldn't see how my life had improved from what it was like before I was cut down; to become the cross Yesu had to carry.

Many seasons passed as I was shunted around from place to place. I saw very little of the world around me, mostly watched the comings and goings of carpenters making chairs, tables, cradles and shelves out of wood I couldn't identify. It seemed I was forgotten like a Great Great Grandfather, until one rainy night the main door into the shed was left open and I saw streaks of light flashing across the sky. It wasn't lightning and I was sure I had never seen anything like that before, plus I heard an akk akk sound. I and others were bundled into a vehicle with no windows. We seemed to travel very slowly at first but rarely hit any bumps. By this time I had become used to others packed tightly next to me and I realised that just maybe I would still have a life; just as Angel said I would. I became aware of a purring sound I couldn't place. Eventually we stopped as dawn crept softly across the land. I and others were hauled out into a yard by men wearing uniforms I didn't recognize. However, I would become familiar with them in the days to come. I caught a glimpse of fields, some yellow, some green dotted with small white fluffy animals. This yard had two large sheds leading off it and various machines. One had enormous wheels on top of which was a seat behind which it dragged great spikes. Other vehicles of similar size stood idly by and I was overcome by a strong smell within the yard. This I worked out emanated from large legged black and white animals making a peculiar sound. The whole picture struck me as strange as the yard was being hosed down by a long tube washing all the muck away from our area.

Close by another odd looking vehicle backed towards us. It was the colour of dirty brown. In the front sat a man whilst others placed us onto a tray. Two men jumped in beside us and a third let down the sides, which appeared to be made of some dark heavy cloth. These he fixed to the sides and pulled up the end of the tray so that we didn't fall out. One of the men knocked on the panel between us and the driver, which seemed to signify we were to get going. This I had never seen before. I learnt later that every vehicle we travelled in, small or large had an engine which took the place of bullocks, and other animals. It could speed up or slow down depending on the driver. As the days wore on I discovered I was in England towards the end of a war. I saw numerous men and women wearing uniforms of various colours, faces full of sorrow but a determination to make the best of things. Buildings flattened and in the rubble, youngsters playing with sticks pretending to shoot each other. All this and more as I was transported here and there. Finally we came to the village of Milton Abbas, well just outside, and although I call it a village it was like no other. For a start there were no shops, just a row of white cottages on either side of the road, a church and a guest house. I had the occasion to see around me. The village was surrounded by high banks from which grew all kinds of trees none of which I had seen before, their leaves changing colour as it was the end of summer. Later that day I caught a glimpse of a very large church perched high above the village which I discovered was called an abbey. Towards the evening men came and placed me within a shed full of shavings, several benches and the sound of a saw. I looked around at my neighbours none of which took any notice of me. To them I was a refugee usurping their home. I wanted to cry out but I didn't know enough of English to make myself understood. Night fell and again I was once more on my own in a strange place. Past memories collided with the present. Seeing the hillside where I grew up with my canopy so tall, the grass, wild flowers and the beauty of the early mornings, sunset and gentle rain. To be housed in sheds for millennia. Fixed in buildings and never to see other trees, the sun or watch little animals and birds; oh!

So long, so long to be cooped up inside warehouses. All I ever experienced were dark stone buildings never to see the daylight properly or feel the warmth of the sun. What now? What next? I shall never be beautiful again. Put me outside to rot. Where at least I can see the sky and stars once more.

He that showed thee, O man what is good;
What doth the Lord require of thee,
But to do justly and to love mercy and to walk
humbly with thy God.
Micah 6:8

Chapter 4

I can hear bells ringing but as yet can see very little whilst propped up in this vast shed. What now? What next? I look around and see all manner of tools. On the far wall of the shed there are oddly shaped sticks, fitted at the bottom with a tiny black substance I had never seen before. Half way up the stick protruded a small, smoothed down piece of wood and attached to the top a padded piece of leather. They were of different lengths and tied in twos. I was mystified as to what use they could be. One morning an enormous log arrived which took up the length of the floor. He was lighter in colour to me and I watched his bark being stripped away. He didn't look too kindly at this treatment and went quite pale.

I wondered if I had been forgotten but on that very day two men carted me to a bench, well what was left of me and gently laid me down. There was much discussion as to what they were about to do. A measuring tape was moved back and forth from my top to my toe. One man referred to a pad he was carrying, checking the figures. His hands glided up and down my torso. I heard music playing from another bench and thought how calming it was and hoped the pale log felt better. It was like nothing I had heard before. The instruments were different from my last home and I felt if I could sing I would hum along. Markings were made close to my edge. The hands felt strong but nothing like the hands of Yesu. I still remember them even now, centuries later.

I watched a machine tear down my side so quickly that the shock of it didn't register straight away. The pain came in waves, my only comfort remembering Angel's words, 'All will be well' This is what I was born for! Gradually the core pain died away and I fell into a trance. I knew I was now in two pieces and likely to be cut in three. Hands lifted me up and did all manner of things to me. I watched my side piece being planed and levelled down smoothed, varnished and moulded one end into a kind of knob. It was now my turn and as I felt all manner of tools I noticed I was gently moulded either side, varnished and stood up to dry. I suppose I had what people would call a 'complete makeover.' As the day wore on I dreamt once more of being beautiful; beautiful within and without. I let go my fear of pain, identity and anger. My spirit soared as I felt being turned inside out – to what end I knew not. Looking across at my outer side and back at myself, I finally understood that I was made up of spiritual and earthly matter; both important to nourish. My spiritual self would live on to eternity and my earthly self would fulfil my calling on this planet. In a peculiar way we were not divided. We could always communicate wherever we went. Although feeling decidedly shaky at this turn of events I knew I could call upon Angel when I needed reassurance, when frightened or in despair. It was like a revelation and I began to actually be thankful that of all the trees to be the cross I was chosen to do so. So many experiences, so much I'd had to learn, above all to trust. Angel's words resounded again, 'All will be well.' Now I was ready to serve.

I felt a surge of life power go from me into 'Stick' and knew then this was the last purge. No more would I be subject to cuts and changes. I was complete for whatever place I was to go. My earthly life, my thoughts, my worries transferred to 'Stick'. My body became my spiritual half, beautifully shaped and shining like the sun.

I looked at 'Stick' who had been moved to the front of our shed where all was for sale. 'Stick' had a shaped head and a foot covered in what I knew now to be a rubber sock glued to his pointy end. There were a great many objects displayed to help the wounded and other service men. A glass door fitted with a bell rang as people came to try out the various devices. I watched as a bright red car pulled up outside, its top folded down and two young men clambered out, the one helping the other. They wore leather jackets lined with fluffy wool, the white showing at the wrists and on the stand up collar.

'Afternoon,' said the one with a limp towards a man behind the counter.' I'm looking for some crutches and a walking stick.' My ears pricked up at this remark.

'I think I can help you there, Sir.'

And so various crutches were tried out, until the young man spied, 'Stick'. He ran his hands up and down feeling the smooth finish, hobbled around the shop and with a big smile said, 'I'll take this one, he's just right.' Money was handed over.

'You'll not be sorry Sir. Great choice.'

And with that the companion uttered, 'Come my Lord,' and together they clambered back into the red car. I watched as it roared away, happy knowing that as a walking stick life would be full of great adventures for a small part of me.

Later that night I called Angel.

'Why have I been polished and shined only to be stored in this place?'

What's so awful about that?

'I've lost all my branches and parts of me and I've spent more time in carpenters hands than I can remember!'

God has fashioned you for a purpose. Your core or soul if you like is now ready for this work. Walking Stick will carry on your earthly existence. Have patience Oak and all will be revealed.

'Where am I to go?'

In God's time He will place you exactly where He wants you to be.

'You mean no more rough handling? No more whittling down in dusty Sheds?'

Exactly.

'You mean I will be a blessing to people in need? Really?...and I am beautiful in God's eyes?'

Stay humble Oak. You have little need of me, so I bid you farewell, from now on I shall come when Walking Stick calls. He has many years of service. You will meet up again and you will know all that there is to know.

Not long after my final talk with Angel I was gently wrapped in a soft material, stored for a while to ponder all that Angel said and finally found myself being transferred to my last resting place.

For a thousand years in your sight are but as yesterday
when it is past
And as a watch in the night.
Psalm 90:4

Chapter 5

I am a walking stick, physically strong and slim. I was amazed that I could still see, hear, and feel. Lying next to my new master I felt the throb of the car's engine. I saw above and beyond as we whizzed along past other vehicles, roads, lanes and buildings. My master winces at each jolt and mutters under his breath. The crutches bounce along on the back seat and the driver attempts to clear the wind screen with his sleeve as it begins to rain. We pull up in a siding with wild flowers peeping out from a hedge and an enormous bank on either side of the road. Above us are trees with their branches entwined. It is like being in a green tunnel. Oh how beautiful to my eyes. The driver clambers out to release a roof top, guiding it over our heads then slips a fastener. Suddenly it is dark inside and conversation between my master and his friend is kept to a minimum. We stop in a village and the driver wanders off, I can only assume requesting directions, for then we are at a building with peculiar hoses, on the ends of which a gadget pours some strange liquid into the side of our car. I was quite intrigued. My master points to a stone building with lots of flowers out the front whilst the driver finishes with the hose. We park around the back and my master leans heavily on me as he clambers out, releasing the roof.

Eventually we arrive in a warm room which is full of laughing men, tables covered with tall glasses, a long raised counter and the occasional dog. I learn this is a pub. All the seats seem to be occupied but the landlord came around to my master and led us to a recess built of bricks with two seats either side of a roaring fire.

'All's well, Sir.'

Our driver appears looking rather wet.

'The usual, Julian.' my master states quietly. He removes his jacket and I see wings sewn onto his grey uniform. Julian brings two large glasses of golden liquid across and the other patrons raise their glasses towards my master who returned their welcome by a nod. An iron hook on the wall close by was where Julian hung their jackets. I heard numerous words which were new to me. Words such as airman, pilots, bombs, batman, pub and 'ploughmans' although I'm not too sure of the last one. Overall it seemed the atmosphere was warm and friendly.

I listened carefully and understood we were in for a long drive to a place called Abinger in Surrey which was where my new master lived. And so we left the pub and continued our drive. A map was poured over and various roads pointed to as the clouds rolled away and a watery sun caused the rain drops to glisten. The roof was kept on as a breeze had picked up. I listened to the conversation but could not work out much of it. Eventually we passed through a place called Bletchingley on the Dorking road to Abinger. Finally we drove up a long crunchy pathway and stopped in front of a large house – I discovered it was called a manor. I saw a church that had been almost completely destroyed. Later I was to learn the history of this village and to see the damage as my master walked all around making notes of what needed to be repaired. World War 2 was over, but with so much desecration it was left to those still standing to repair their surroundings.

My master had great difficulty reaching the top of the steps, he leaned heavily on me and for a moment I thought we would both fall down. The door flew open and a smiling lady embraced my master.

'Charles,' she whispered. 'Thank God.'

At her feet was an animal with floppy ears running around in circles. And then a larger animal appeared nuzzling up to Charles' hand. The driver, carrying the crutches and a large canvas bag, brought up the rear and Charles indicated to him where to put them down. That was another word I learnt; the bag was called a holdall.

'Come in, come in there's sure to be a cup of tea going! Isn't that right, Mother?' Charles said, raising an eyebrow to the woman.

'It's Julian isn't it?' She held out her hand. 'Of course do stay awhile, you must be tired both of you. Thank you for looking after my son.'

'Well if it's no bother...' He smiled, following Charles, me, his mother and the two animals into a room which had enormous windows looking over a large lawn in need of attention and an area with white lines painted on the grass and a net strung across it. So we sat, Charles with me clasped to his hand. A maid appeared carrying a tray with cake, cups and saucers, plates and a small jug containing milk, a teapot and a bowl containing little lumps of sugar to be clasped by an implement called tongs, which was easier said than done by Julian. I discovered Julian came from the village and was the family chauffeur. Charles' father sat in The House of Lords (whatever that meant). Charles was responsible for the welfare of the people who lived in the village cottages and the care of its church, school and neighbourhood. Charles had been away for some time with Julian as his bat man. Julian stood up to leave saying, 'If you're not needing me, My Lady, Sir, I'll be off.'

'The Daimler is still in the garage, it has hardly been used since you've been away in the Air Force, what with petrol rationing! Now that Charles is back and His Lordship is in London, it would be a good time to take a few days off Julian. Get some rest.' Gently she added, 'I saw your mother not so long ago. I expect she will be very pleased to have you to herself for a bit.'

'Sir?' Julian queried to Charles.

'Absolutely. Take a few days off. I shan't be going anywhere soon. Now I need a bit of shut eye!' Charles waved his hand and touching his leg sighed. With that Julian let himself out the back way. I guessed he lived close by.

So that was my first day in Abinger, my first night in a real house, and my first encounter with Blondie and Beatrice.

For a while my life became very busy. Charles needed me to climb the sweeping staircase up to his bedroom. Most of the time he used me to walk around the house until he grew tired and then he used the crutches so then I was stood back into the hall stand. From here I saw all number of people who came to the manor. Not long after I arrived a young woman named Avril visited; she and Charles spent time in the conservatory.

As Charles began to walk around Abinger checking on what needed to be done in the aftermath of war he ventured into Abinger Bottom with me and Blondie. These forays required driving his red car with Blondie and me sharing the passenger seat. The weather was quite cold but the short journey was a delight. We would pass a few cottages tucked away in the forest, in front of which ran a small stream. Then he would drive up a small incline, dropping down the other side towards two houses nestled at the bottom, one of which belonged to Avril's family. We'd alight on a flat courtyard and Avril would come out to meet us from a much weathered front door; followed by Bracken, a dog with longish red hair. It would seem Bracken and Blondie were good friends as we strolled through the coppice bordering a lane that led to a public house. Many hours were passed in this fashion. The rest of the time was taken up with Charles talking with tradesmen within the damaged church of St James. That's where I learnt it had been hit by a flying bomb during the recent war.

Hardly a day went by between the warmer and winter months of that year when Charles did not collect me from the hall stand. It was an unusual feeling to be used as his help mate. Gone were the years of being shut away in some shed, being stripped down, and gone were my anxieties. Sometimes I thought of Oak and wondered where he was, especially at the end of an exciting day when returned to the hall stand. During the following months I learnt many words and understood what was happening around me. Charles' father died of influenza; his mother handed over the manor house and moved into the Gate Lodge down at the start of the drive way. Charles married Avril at St.

Andrews Church of England at Sonning, on the River Thames in Berkshire, as their local church of St James was still far from being fully repaired. I learnt many things each day but above all my life as a walking stick was worth something after all.

If we hope for that we see not, then do we with patience wait for it.
Romans 8:25

Chapter 6

During those early days Charles attended many a church service and re-union with his squadron. I loved the walks through country where all manner of trees grew. Sometimes the ground was covered with blue flowers and at other times tall stemmed yellow flowers with trumpet like centres nodded as we passed by. Bracken and Blondie sniffed through the foliage picking up the scent of squirrels. I found myself hearing a whisper on a regular basis that gave me the names of plants and trees. And so not only did I learn words, I felt within myself a point to my existence.

Not long after Charles married Avril we drove up to London and I saw many bombed sights. One that I recall especially, was The Guards Chapel at Wellington Barracks. It had been hit twice, the second in 1944 when over two hundred people were attending morning service; half were killed and the rest injured. By the late 1950's repairs had been made and Charles attended a communion service. I wasn't sure what this entailed but to my surprise I watched as the congregation walked towards the altar. Each person knelt to receive a small piece of bread and a sip of wine from a silver chalice. A small child put her hands on the alter rail. She was crying as the vicar placed his hands on her head murmuring words of comfort. Charles knelt next to her and hooked me over the rail. I saw numerous hands touching the rail and felt a frisson of recognition and a sense of joy as I realised Oak had become a beautiful sight. He was beaming with light and colour. Oh to be re-united was a blessing in itself as I watched the many praying hands receiving the bread and wine. This was what he was born to do, giving comfort in this modern age, reaching back to the hillside from where he was born. I remembered Angel's words whilst lying in the snow all those years ago, 'All will be well.' I looked upwards at the cross above the alter and it dawned on me that the bread offered to the people represented the body of Yesu and the wine his blood. All those centuries ago - with the march of time Yesu still lived for those who followed his message to 'Love one another.' I wanted to cry out, to tell the people what part Oak and I played. It seemed such a short time to be reunited and I so wanted to stay there resting next to Oak.

Charles was made a Peer of the Realm following in his father's footsteps. In time, their first son arrived and was named Adam. He attended Marlborough College in Wiltshire and seven years later a second son, David, was born. The days for me merged into each other as did the dinner parties where I heard many a conversation around the dining table as guests discussed the common market and later the European Union. Neither of these things I fully understood except the changes caused a lot of angst for farmers. During these dinners Charles kept me by his side. The boys would question their parents as to what was discussed after the guests had left. The boys brought different friends to the manor due to their age difference and their personalities. Adam was keen on cars, planes and engines - in fact anything that moved fast, whereas David preferred quieter pursuits. He loved drawing and many of his nature sketches were displayed along the kitchen walls which I would see when Charles returned from his walks.

Following in his brother's footsteps as a pupil of Marlborough College, whilst on the train David spied a white horse carved into the chalk hillside. From that moment he was hooked on horses and begged Charles for one of his own. As a little fellow he first had a pony. I was taken out of the hall stand to watch him riding around in an enclosure led by a groom. Charles was very keen watching David grow up and later bought him a mount of his own.

As the years passed Adam enjoyed racing cars and David became part of the equestrian team gaining notable success. I spent a longer time in the hall stand as Charles had little need of me except when he and Avril walked around the estate. He was busy with electricians, plumbers and various tradesmen renovating the eastern wing of the manor so that he and Avril could spend their retirement in comfort. As they entertained less Avril spent her days in the herb garden, and joined the local dramatic society. One evening Charles received a call which shook him to the core. Avril went into shock. Adam had died in a car crash. It was pouring with rain on the day of the funeral and I had to share my home with many a wet umbrella. Guests came to comfort the family in their sorrow. Two weeks later David had a nasty fall taking a difficult jump at a meet. He broke his collar bone and right leg in two places. His dreams of equestrian glory were equally shattered.

Charles and Avril decided to go abroad for a while and left a skeleton staff to keep the household running and a manager in charge of the general running of the estate. He left me behind but I didn't mind.

I was once more called into service, but for David now and life became more interesting once again. Eight years after his accident, David was voted into Parliament as a member of the Tory party, following in his grandfather's footsteps.

Various Prime Ministers came and went, John Major, Tony Blair, David Cameron, Theresa May and finally Boris Johnson. In these latter days there were a great many arguments about leaving the European Union.

But what did a Prime Minister do, I wondered? What did all those people do who sat on the long forms facing each other and argued about matters that seemed to be of such great importance? What were constituents?' and what was an election? What was sterling? So many things I didn't understand. I knew what I did had helped Charles and now David get about. I could prove I was a help as my foot plate had worn out and I needed another. I hoped it would be made of something softer as the pain of jarring each time I was banged onto the ground was getting too much to bear. Not to mention the times I fell onto the ground. Completely shook me up.

By now Charles and Avril feeling their age hardly ventured outside the manor so I was pleased David needed me. He moved into his grandfather's apartment in London as the House was sitting at very late hours. As we drove through London I noticed many new buildings where all the rubble had been and new vehicles, so different from all those years ago. It was an eye opener to me as when I first was taken to London so many buildings had been bombed. I wondered if David would take me to the Guards Chapel where I could touch Oak again but this was not going to happen.

So here I was in London; the year 2020 and I was surrounded by noise and very little relief. Sometimes he took me to St. James' park when he wanted to think things over. The best time was when we went down to the manor for the occasional weekend – there things had changed. Various staff now managed the grounds, new people moved into the cottages. Some cottages were in private hands now as some of the land surrounding the manor had been sold off; but not the stables. They were fast becoming a business. I saw small men riding various horses and wearing bright colours now and again. They were called jockeys, and the horses were very valuable with stable hands looking after them in the yard. Like his father before him David checked on a regular basis his horses, the stables and riders. Whereas Charles used to take me around the estate checking on what needed to be done, David took me down to watch the rides. I missed Blondie, Bracken and Beatrice who had long ago passed away, and I rarely saw Avril or Charles. I realised nothing stayed the same, people grew older, had accidents, went away, died, causing untold misery to those they loved and left behind; whereas I remained the same – just a walking stick.

I was feeling rather battered and tired. Standing in the hall stand I took stock of my foot and nicks along my shaft. On this particular evening I noticed I was sharing the hall stand with a rather shiny black walking stick who looked at me with disdain, there were also two umbrellas dripping water over the tiled floor and down by my foot. I don't know how I am to keep going; no one has taken any notice of my plight.

'Angel, are you there?'

It's been some time since we last had a chat.

'I am worn down with aches and pains .It is so degrading sharing my home with these others. They don't take any notice of me. I was here first.'

You are going to need to share. The world as you know it is going through great change.

'You can say that again. I don't get what is happening. Members of Parliament sacked then re-instated. David Cameron, a past Prime Minister was shocked so many people wanted to leave the European Union. See I have kept my nose down and tried to understand what is going on. But then there have been more elections and dates thrown around so that my head spins and my foot is a mess.'

There will be more upheavals and scandals before all is finalised. There are still things for you to do and lessons to learn.

'I wish I had never left Oak's side. He is now beautiful once again and at peace.'

There will come a time when no-one will touch an alter rail or even attend a church service; so very few people will be kneeling at alter rails anywhere in the world.

'Oh my!'

Rest, Walking Stick. You are going to travel to your homeland once more. Shortly after your visit you will hear of floods, roaring fires, wild storms, earthquakes and a pandemic.

'I don't know that word.'

Trust me. I shall be here for you when you call and I will give you rest .Your journey is coming to an end in all its glory.

And so it came about my foot was cleansed and a new sock attached. I found myself in a flying machine called a plane with my master David. He took a holiday whilst parliament was suspended and we arrived in Israel. Here he took me everywhere each day with a group of people that were staying in the same hotel. Some places gave me a jolt; I can't explain why except to say even the air itself triggered memories. I felt immediately at home which may have been due to recognizing the long robes and head gear some men were wearing – they seemed familiar in some way. There were other strange sights, men wearing all black caftans with enormous hats. They seemed to be praying against a wall. Their hair was curled down the side of their faces bouncing about as they dipped up and down. I wondered what the group made of it all. Guards in uniforms were carrying heavy weapons all around as people from many countries watched this spectacle. One stared at David and me the entire time we were there but nothing happened. They could see he needed me to stand. I learnt later that this was known as the Wailing Wall a remnant of the Jewish temple. As I watched some of them put prayers between the cracks in the wall. They were Orthodox Jews. It was a strange sight indeed. Each evening our guide explained what we would see the next day, which appeared to be places Yesu had visited to preach and heal the people all those years ago.

One morning the bus took us to Jericho and another day to Bethlehem, but the morning I'll never forget was when the bus stopped in the hills of Galilee. Here I nearly fainted as we got off the bus. I saw many oak trees. Some tourists sat among the slopes of grass and wild flowers. Some removed from their shoulders a strap that had a box like object which they held up to their eyes moving their fingers up and down, and some just stood breathing in the air looking down towards the Sea of Galilee. I wanted David to lie on the grass with me so that I could look up to the trees, so I could watch the birds and feel the ground and its creatures underneath. But this didn't happen; instead he used me to trace a circle across the ground as he leant against an oak tree. I could have wept for he leant down and picked up an oak fruit putting it in his pocket. One of the tourists joked watching him do this, 'Going to grow oaks on your lands are we David? Should imagine you'd need more than one acorn!'

That night I recalled the time Oak was cut down and how we were pulled by ropes and tossed in a cart drawn by oxen. The shock, the humiliation, to end up on a midden with Yesu nailed to us all those years ago. Of course that place has changed through the centuries as has the authenticity of Yesu's birth place, burial and tomb. And here was I scaled down to a mere walking stick and Oak living miles away as an alter rail in London! I thought of calling Angel in my distress but there was too much in my mind to organize my thoughts properly. As we visited more sights I began to understand that this country, my country, was nowadays generally called the Holy Land. This was the Jewish homeland and people returned from all over the world to claim this land as theirs.

Every night the group sat in a circle reading passages from a book. Each person had one and they called it a Bible. I listened and was amazed to hear it was about Yesu. The day Yesu carried His cross, His teaching and that He did this for the whole world, which meant not only Jewish people but Muslims and other religions. That was why I had seen people wearing small crosses around their necks, crosses sewn into robes, crosses in churches on grave stones and being sold from stalls around the streets. It was all because of Yesu's crucifixion so many eons ago. I was there with oak. We heard His teaching to forgive and love one another. From my perspective there was little of that throughout the world. Most people did not love each other or try to understand each other within their own nations so how could they love others? I decided to ask Angel about this and why this was so. It was time to pack and return to England.

No sooner were we on the plane back to London than His Lordship took papers out of his briefcase to read and also an object called a tablet where he tapped letters at great speed. On arrival at Heathrow Airport, (I am still learning new words daily and amazed at how this can be;) we were met by our chauffeur. No longer Julian of course, now it was a man called Thomas. It was a mystery to me how Thomas knew when to meet us.

Instead of going back to the manor we went straight to the London apartment where David left his suitcase before being whisked to the Houses of Parliament. This time there were crowds of people yelling and waving around signs; some seemed angry but most were waving the Union flag.

'I need to get back for the vote, Thomas. No more extensions. The deal has to be approved so that we leave the EU by January 31,' he said.

'God bless us, Sir, get back our country! The Queen has given her Royal Consent?'

'Aye. I have things to say in the House. Just look at all these people lining the streets.'

I found myself once more inside Parliament, listening to conversations left and right of me. And then my master was given the floor as they say. A hush came upon everyone present. Leaning on me, David stood up.

'Mr Speaker. Whatever happens, the Prime Minister must ensure that we have complete control of our fishing waters.'

'Hear hear,' came from all those present.

'And that there is no question of a level playing field between Britain and the EU when it comes to trade deals with other countries.' He sat down to a great deal of noise. I think I remember most of what took place. The vote was taken to loud applause and so was carried. Outside people were cheering as we were driven back to the apartment. I could see my master was exhausted as he prepared for bed. I didn't know what to think; once more confused as to the ways of man. On January 31 2020 Britain would apparently leave the European Union and what that would mean was beyond my understanding, but my master seemed relieved. I wasn't ready to call Angel and listen to what he would say.

Angel was right about scandals in high places. As my master watched the news from a box called a television whilst I was leaning against his chair, there were numerous occasions when he tut-tutted. A tourist business of long standing and prestige had to call in the receivers. One of the Queen's favourite sons got caught up in a scandal by being friends with a rich tycoon who allegedly procured young women for his friends. The Prince felt it his duty to refuse an honour from the Queen. Then a grandson of the Queen married a divorced commoner, which on the surface was straight forward enough. However, it seemed then he was persuaded by his wife to forgo his role as a Prince and move away from England. That was discussed in great detail. I had so many questions to ask Angel that I didn't know where to begin. This modern world was beyond my understanding. I longed to be with Oak and his peaceful, restored situation. Little did I know what else was to come.

Many people across the world were caught up in raging fires which decimated their land and houses. As a result of this quite a number of people suffered from the smoke and died. Violent storms smashed dwellings and flooded areas which made it difficult for people to get to higher ground. Every day I listened to David reading aloud from his newspaper which he dropped off to his neighbour, an elderly man in the apartment next door. Climate change was a topic of conversation, whatever that meant. David would drive himself down to the manor at weekends and walk across fields with me and sometimes go into the local church, now fully restored, and just sit. By Sunday afternoon he would join the throngs of people driving back to London and our usual routine of going to the Houses of Parliament.

When the Oak tree is felled, the whole forest echoes
with it; but a hundred
Acorns are planted silently by some unnoticed breeze.
Thomas Carlyle

Chapter 7

I longed for the peace of the Manor House and at last David drove down to Abinger, planting me in the hall stand. My luck was in; the black shiny stick was nowhere in sight. David went off to speak with his housekeeper in the kitchen. There was a weak sun shining through from the high window in the hall and everything was quiet. I took a moment to reflect on events. David returned, picking up his mail from a silver tray on a table against the furthest wall and retired to his study without the need of me. Now was the time to call Michael.

Peace be with you Walking Stick.

'I can do with that. My mind can't take any more shocks. I am quite exhausted! I much prefer the manor house to the apartment as I don't like the smells at breakfast or the cities fumes.'

What is worrying you?

'Well...' sighing, I said, 'What is this Brexit thing? And why do people argue so?'

It is the nature of man to control others; to gain power.

'To fight?'

Yes, to fight

'You mean to take what others have and to keep what is theirs?'

In a way. In this Brexit situation a majority of people feel that they are being forced to act by how another country tells them to. They decided they have had enough of that. They do not want to be told by another how to spend their money and what they must give up.

'So people here voted to go it alone so to speak – pull out of their original agreement. Is that it?'

You could say that. You are hearing a great many complex situations.

'Is that why I find it hard to understand what is right?'

There is no right or wrong answer Walking Stick. It's all a matter of how you think.

'Life for me was so easy being part of Oak on that hillside thousands of years ago. I can't explain the feeling I had returning to my roots in Israel. The wild flowers, the light, in a sense the timeless atmosphere. I so wanted to just lie down on the hill side forever and think of nothing.'

You've been privileged Walking Stick with a long and full life helping others. Useful to others in their need. Did you know that King Charles the second once hid in an enormous Oak tree when his country was at civil war. The Round Heads they were called and they didn't agree with many of the laws Charles made.

'Why was that?'

The general public were very poor and they felt Charles lived an extravagant life. He took their lands keeping the people poor. Also people were divided in their worship. A lot of wealth was spent on elaborate churches whereas the people needed food. So Charles hid in an Oak tree by day in the grounds of Boscombe House in Shropshire, climbing down to his bed in the house at night. There are many oaks all around England but none more so than in Shropshire, which is not far from where you live. There are many public houses called the Royal Oak in villages scattered about England.

'Oh my! How did they get here?'

They have been here for centuries.

'I didn't know that. I did see a cousin in a London park when David took a walk but I wasn't aware of any others. I need to think about what you've just said. Oaks all around the world! I can't believe it? There would be more of us in England?'

Yes, and many a story as to what they have achieved. I will tell you about them sometime.

And with that he faded from sight. I felt humbled by his remarks and felt quite downcast resting in the hall stand, my mind trying to understand my position in the world and what would be in store for me.

Not long after my encounter with Angel, David took me back to London where he was dealing with people, papers, general meetings and the future plans for the economy.

The fruit of the righteous is a tree of life;
And he that winneth souls is wise.
Proverbs 11:30

Chapter 8

I didn't sleep well that night pondering all that Angel told me. Was I really only just a tiny part of the universe? I had thought I was more important than any other wood. I wondered if Oak knew that his earthly life had been fashioned as to what man decided. My life too. I was quite insignificant. This had never occurred to me before. I wanted to talk things over with Oak but this wasn't going to happen. How easy were our early years and how pleasant. So much had happened to us and the world since. I felt quite overwhelmed.

The following day I was in for a surprise or shock whichever way you look at it. David drove into a town close by with me in the passenger seat. We entered a most unusual shop, one I didn't recall ever having been into before. Along one side were wooden frames and odd looking stands. Many coloured tubes next to coloured pots, some material in rolls and all manner of paper, clips and the suchlike, also bottles of some liquid which had a strong smell to them. On the counter were brushes tied up in bundles, likewise pencils and charcoal. It was a mystery to me why David should avail himself of all these objects. He stumbled out of the shop carrying a huge parcel and leaning on me.

Returning to the manor he deposited all that he had bought into a large airy room attached to the house but its entrance concealed by a bookcase in his study. Entry was by pushing a button next to the book case which revealed a doorway as it slid to the side. I was propped up against the wall from which we entered and I could see the garden and grassy slope through a large picture window at the far end. Of all my time in this house and I had never been in here before.

There were paintings and sketches scattered around, some leaning against the wall of the house and some drawings of villages and churches arranged on a desk. There was a stool, pallets, paint brushes, paint pots coloured tubes, rags and glass jars. Two large easels in the middle of the room took up a fair size of this, 'art studio' as I heard it referred to. I felt quite dizzy from a similar smell to the shop we had visited. Shortly after dropping off his art supplies David took me down to the stables for which I was thankful – even though there was a strong smell here too, but combined with the fresh air it was more to my liking. More earthy somehow.

The next few weeks David spent his time between what is called 'the Chamber' and his office in London, firmly arguing Britain's withdrawal from the European Union. Apparently it wasn't as simple as I thought. Many a day we entered a local pub which was very noisy as he stared into space drinking a long golden liquid with a frothy substance on the top. I could tell he was exhausted and not in the mood to play darts, cards or socialising. First thing in the morning he would take me to a park and read aloud from an early edition of a daily newspaper with me propped up against the seat. I would try to understand as he read snippets about Brexit and the horrors of a pandemic. More to my liking were the buds opening high up in the surrounding canopy. Small wild flowers lifted their heads to the early morning sun and I thought again that I once had an easy life just like them. Birds of all kinds seemed to be busy calling and fluttering among the leaves and many a person ran by. Winter had finally given way to Spring. Of course some days were cloudy – even raining, but there was an atmosphere of hope that this small island would come through in the end, confounding the critics.

It was coming up to the Easter festival, a time of renewal, of gambling lambs, baby chickens and chocolate eggs wrapped in all manner of colours. Whilst David stopped by a shop window I saw cards displayed with flowers, butterflies and messages of good will. Suddenly I saw a few cards with a cross on the front, usually in the centre. Some were painted gold with Yesu pinned to the cross beam. I found these images quite disturbing and quite extraordinary. Why would anyone send a card with a cross on it – it was a terrible thing full of agony and shame. I didn't want to be reminded of it.

I heard snippets of conversation about chocolate, a long weekend and a bank holiday. Oh and there was mention of Good Friday where everything closed down and people took a holiday. No one said why it was called Good Friday and I thought it was all very confusing. What was it all about?

The evenings prior to the thing I would know as the pandemic were generally quiet, but as the weeks went by the phone sitting atop of some books kept ringing. I found this disturbing. David was sprawled out in the armchair reading a newspaper and half watching a programme on the television. I understood it was called *Who do you think you are?'* where people traced their family tree back as far as they could. I felt a small affinity with them as they discovered what their ancestors lives were like. The shocks, the tears, their pride was all visible but none had experienced my life as part of an Oak tree from way back in time. I was still living –if only just, and Oak was fulfilling his destiny.

One sunny morning David was at his desk as were most Members of Parliament. The building was abuzz with noise and I longed to be taken to the park. He received a message from the Prime Minister to discuss further issues on Brexit so he grasped me and some papers and arrived at the Prime Minister's door. I saw other members also making their way down the corridor to the room. We gathered around as the door opened and David, like the others, greeted the Prime Minister who was sitting behind a long oval desk. All eyes were on Boris Johnson as members sat down around the table. He looked rather flushed but smiling. As he began to speak he started to have a coughing fit. Fumbling for his handkerchief at the same time he waved a small blue book for everyone to see. I gathered everyone recognised it for what it was. There were smiles all around and hand clapping.

'After thirty years we have our own passport back again. Those of you who need to travel please apply for a British passport as quickly as you can…and ditch your EU one!'

With that he rose, excusing himself amidst much laughter and smiles all round. It was one of those defining moments that seemed to create energy in the gathered members, knowing the work still required to tackle all the issues which lay before them in returning sovereignty to Britain once again. There was some discussion as members filed out back to their offices. David stayed behind waiting for the Prime Minister to return.

'Are you alright Prime Minister?'

Boris sat down, pouring a glass of water, 'There is much to be done, David.' And with that he launched into various topics, most of which I had no understanding. There was something about the cost of health and its issues interspersed with a word; pandemic. This, I remember, was the first time I had heard that talked about. Apparently it appeared to be sweeping the world. Tests for a virus would have to be organised as it could be passed from person to person, like an unseen enemy sweeping through populations and no vaccine to defend against it in sight.

Within a fortnight people would be advised to stay at home, stay away from others, be careful as to what they touched and if they felt unwell to present themselves to their nearest doctor. This was called 'Lock down'.

There seemed to be an enormous amount of activity as members discussed among themselves what was happening to many countries around the world. How each were handling this health disaster. Yet in London, red busses, cars, taxis and people all went about their usual business. Offices at noon emptied of their workers during their lunch hour to visit restaurants, parks, cafes and pubs. Trains filled with shoppers and commuters. In the evening David returned to the apartment after visiting the local pub for a pint of that golden liquid and then he watched the news on television. But it wasn't long before planes and ships were rumoured to have carried the virus from overseas; their passengers bewildered by health officials checking if they had brought the virus with them.

People began to panic buy supplies before they were forced to stay home and of course shops ran out of essentials. Fights broke out and some took advantage of the situation by buying up large quantities of basics, then selling them privately at much higher prices.

At the same time winter was over. The skies were blue. Buds were once more opening to all shades of green amongst trees. Spring flowers were in abundance and the word 'holiday' was banded around.

Keep right on to the end of the road
Keep right on to the end... though the road be long
Let your heart be strong... keep right on to the end.
Harry Lauder

Chapter 9

As usual, David still took me to a local park and read aloud from the early edition of the newspaper. I leaned against his leg and tried to understand snippets about the horrors of the pandemic. On this particular morning there was a picture of the Queen and her encouraging words.

'Never give up, never despair.'

Similar to the words of Sir Winston Churchill spoken seventy five years ago during World War 2. David muttered these and other words, humming songs from that time.

It crossed my mind we would not be visiting any more parks for a while. I felt so sad. Shops, pubs and entertainment venues were soon to close. In fact everywhere people met in groups was not allowed. The British public were told to isolate by staying at home. Of course the economy would collapse if no one worked or spent money. It was something the younger generation had never experienced. Who would pay their rent and how were they to obtain food were just a couple of the mystifying questions.

Headlines were banded about from newspapers, 'UK

recession worst for 300 years.'

Thousands were dying and six million jobs would be at risk if the lock down went on too long. I gathered most normal operations were put on hold as there were not enough beds or wards to care for the sick. Extra tent hospitals were erected, safety gowns and masks were needed. Food was to be distributed to the elderly to save them from coming in contact with anyone who had the virus. It was the strangest thing.

The virus spread across the nation. Even the heir to the British throne was not immune. He and his wife moved away from London to isolate themselves in their Scottish home. The Prime Minister stayed home citing he didn't feel well. The next report said he had checked into a London hospital with breathing problems. This was a national disaster. Other countries were having the same problems and all were trying to keep their populations from dying.

Rishi Sunak the Chancellor took over. He unveiled a 30 billion pound safety net. The National Health Service would receive 5 billion pounds covering other most needed public services.

Governments across the world were thrown into panic and I was overwhelmed by all the news. Especially the soaring numbers of sick and dying people. Each evening the television news hardly spoke about anything else. No one was immune to this virus. It was like a war but this time no one saw it coming, and no shots were fired. How could you fight against something you couldn't see or hear?

David continued working from his office looking decidedly unwell and as I predicted, there were no more park outings. We only went back and forth from the apartment to his office. Those who could were asked to work from home. Weddings and funerals were having to cut their numbers severely. Sports teams were stood down and airlines in some countries collapsed. Schools were directed to 'on line' learning. That I found was above my understanding. Maybe it meant that children had to stay home and study. It must have been quite an ordeal for parents and children alike. Thousands of people lost their jobs as soon as the lock down took place. It occurred to me a pandemic was worse than men going to war as in most cases their countries although damaged would eventually recover. But this unseen virus could wipe out complete populations if it wasn't stopped somehow in its tracks. The only defence seemed to be keeping your distance from each other. An impossibility for public travel, and those living in poor surroundings

David decided to return to Abinger and self-isolate.

Driving through London I was struck by how few vehicles were on the road. It was so quiet and where before much of the skyline early in the morning was hazy it now seemed crystal clear. Nearing home he stopped at a chemist and smeared some heady stuff across his hands. Grasping me I felt quite dizzy and wasn't sure if I could stay upright. We returned to the car with his package and then stopped at an off-licence. The same smearing of his hands occurred here. By the time we reached the manor and we climbed the front steps I nearly swooned. Is that how it feels when people drink too much? The smell on my head was overwhelming. I was not looking forward to a repeat. David's housekeeper met us at the doorway. She and David got into some discussion.

I heard her say, '...and churches are closed too.'

Later that evening, whilst propped up in the hall stand, I thought on what she said. Poor Oak, no one would be kneeling at the altar rail, no hands would touch his beautiful self – for how long no one knew. And I expect he would have little idea as to what had happened. How I longed to see him again. I suppose just like human families cut off from each other. I pondered on other cities throughout the world. Like us quiet, with no people, no crowds and no traffic. The corona virus had brought the UK economy to a temporary standstill, and I gathered it had done similar damage worldwide. My head cleared and I was able to rest until the morning.

When the oak tree is felled, the whole forest echoes with it, but a hundred acorns are planted silently by some unnoticed breeze.
Thomas Carlyle

Chapter 10

The days at the manor were very peaceful. David kept to a routine, walking down to the stables in the morning. In the afternoon he set up his easel in the grounds, painting various views of the gardens, trees and swathes of wild flowers. Daisies and clover peeped out across the lawn. I liked their happy faces which according to the gardener needed to be left alone. I don't think David agreed. Snowdrops, I learned, were not wild flowers, their gentle heads facing the earth, nor were the tall daffodils bobbing in the breeze. My favourite place was the wood where a carpet of bluebells stood. I learnt that all these plants grew from bulbs waiting for the Spring sunshine to warm the earth so they could reach up and break through. Much like when oak grew all those years ago.

No one called at the manor, no grand dinners took place. The housekeeper kept her distance, leaving messages in the kitchen; the gardeners waved as we passed by. In the evening David turned on the television in time to hear the Queen say, 'Our streets are not empty, they are filled with the love and care we have for each other.'

Her words of comfort were said on the anniversary of VE Day. Something David understood, I was pleased for him although I had no idea what it meant. He mixed a drink as we listened to further news and smiled to see the Prime Minister fully recovered and back to work. Boris thanked the staff who looked after him. We watched as he left St. Thomas' Hospital saying, 'I owe them my life.' Later, David was relieved to see Boris in front of the cameras again, announcing that his fiancé Carrie had given birth to a son. David immediately contacted the Prime Minister, congratulating him on his recovery and becoming a father.

Rescue packages were put in place to pay the wages of millions of workers as the Prime Minister announced his new 'battle for Britain'. Border patrols were put in place and I gathered no one was allowed to enter the country unless they were returning home from afar – and then went into self-isolation. So much information was broadcast on the television. Even about the millions of people relying on coins and paper money to make their daily payments. From this piece of news I realised there were some people suspicious of notes and coins as though whoever touched them might catch the virus. I longed to talk with Oak regarding all that I was learning about people during this pandemic. The death toll kept rising and I feared for David as he coughed his way throughout the day.

One evening I listened very carefully. Scientists around the world were working to produce a vaccine but it would take a long time before anyone could safely use it. In the meantime the measures already put in place, like self-isolating would have to continue to prevent the virus from spreading. I thought of calling Angel to explain to me what exactly a virus was and how this thing called a vaccine would help, however, I guessed it was a serious issue and my understanding wouldn't help matters.

I did wonder about other things though. What was it like to die? I had only seen one person actually die and that was Yesu all those years go. He was beaten, scourged and nailed to me and Oak. But this was entirely different. People were dying from something you couldn't see. Why would something like this happen? What was the cause? I began to feel anxious myself.

Very early on a sunny morning I was wondering what the day would bring when I was astonished to see David, or should I say His Lordship, coming down the stairs dressed in a checked shirt with his sleeves rolled up. He wore blue trousers and carried a jacket with leather elbow patches over his shoulder with brown boots on his feet. Round his neck was a small yellow scarf. Not his usual city clothes. He was whistling as he collected me and we went around to the back of the manor. Close by was his art studio and a large vehicle which I had never seen before. He unlocked the vehicle and opened it up from the back. There was a door leading out from the studio which I hadn't noticed either. He went back and forth from the studio to the vehicle placing his art supplies, a folding chair and small table in the back. Next we went into the kitchen where he picked up a picnic basket, collected a lightly coloured summer hat from the hall, closed the vehicle back door before opening the driver's door to the vehicle, propped me up on the passenger seat and started the engine. He drove out of the estate and took various roads before driving through Shropshire and passed Boscobel House. As I looked out of the window at the varying countryside it seemed a long way from Surrey. David chuckled as we drove past many trees which I gather as a boy he would have climbed. We drove through Salop, the sun high with hardly a cloud in the sky. We seemed to be the only vehicle driving that day. David drove through a village and past a church behind which was a narrow lane with oak trees forming an arch above us. We came out into the sunshine again climbing a gentle gradient. To our right a green slope dropped away and it was here on a grassy verge near the top he parked the big car. You could see for miles. Close by, growing all around were young oak trees as far as the eye could see. I felt I was in heaven.

David unpacked the car setting up the small table, a box of paints and brushes. He stood a small easel in front of the chair and then opened the picnic case, taking out a flask of coffee and some wrapped sandwiches. The coffee smelt good. He was hungry and ate a sandwich. I was leaning against the easel watching him wiping the paint brushes with a wet cloth, and fixing some canvas on the easel. We must have been there for quite a while for his painting was taking shape; a farmer in the distance riding a tractor, a barn and house vaguely outlined. A kind of energy from the oak trees breathed all around us and into his painting. There were little acorns scattered around and a breeze blew up dislodging his hat. I watched it bouncing down the hillside. David went to grab it knocking the easel and me over. He jumped up, tripping over me, scrambling down the hill after his hat. It seemed a long time before he came back, half crawling. I felt ridiculous on the ground. His hat was rather dirty so he brushed at it but it only made it worse. Eventually he stood up looking around, took a smaller flask from his jacket pocket and drank its contents. Then to my surprise he picked me up and stood me in a hollow of an old oak tree. As I watched him return to his painting the light and warmth were changing. I realised he hadn't coughed since we arrived in Shropshire.

It was early evening as he began packing everything away in the back of the vehicle. I watched him close the back door of the big car expecting him to collect me but he started the engine and drove away. He went back to Abinger without me. Surely he would remember and turn around. Several hours went by, the shadows fell across the land and I snuggled into the tree. I watched the moon and saw the stars for the first time in years and I thought of all the things that had happened in my life. How Oak became an alter rail and me a walking stick and realised that almost anything can be made of oak…there's furniture, cider barrels, baskets, ships, cathedrals; so many objects for man to use. Even acorns fed to pigs to fatten them up. I was content to rest here awhile or even to sleep for all eternity. We had carried the son of God and fulfilled his plan, how special was that.

Several days later I heard a child's voice.

'Grandpa look what I've found!' A young face was beaming at me as I was lifted up and out from the womb of the oak. 'Just what you need,' he said.

A shaky hand ran gently across my head as a pair of pale blue eyes smiled down at me.

...as the acorn is nourished by the dead leaves of the oak, hope strengthens that the rise and fall of men and their movements are only the changing foliage of the ever-growing tree of life, while underneath a greater revolution goes on continually.
Winston Churchill, The River War

Acknowledgements

I thank Hilry Dixon, who spurred me on during lengthy telephone conversations.

Les Guy, my Salvation Army friend, for his encouraging assurance that, 'All will be well.'

I would also like to thank Adam Lancaster, for his technical help in getting the book to the team at Leschenault Press.

And I would, in turn, like to thank Leschenault Press who made 'Cut to Size' possible.

About the Author

Sally Cattell was born in 1942, and spent her childhood in Laleham-on-Thames. She was educated at the Welsh Girls School in Ashford, Middlesex, and from there, attended the Guildhall School of Music and Drama in London.

Marrying an officer in the Australian Army, she emigrated to Australia in 1961. Her background led to working in Radio, Theatre and Script Writing; also teaching in schools, colleges and the University of Tasmania. She directed 'The Diary of Anne Frank', to packed houses at the Theatre Royal in Hobart.

Home is now Queensland's hinterland, she is an Anglican Chaplain at the Gold Coast University Hospital. This is her second book, her first, 'The Stained Glass Window', was published in 2008.